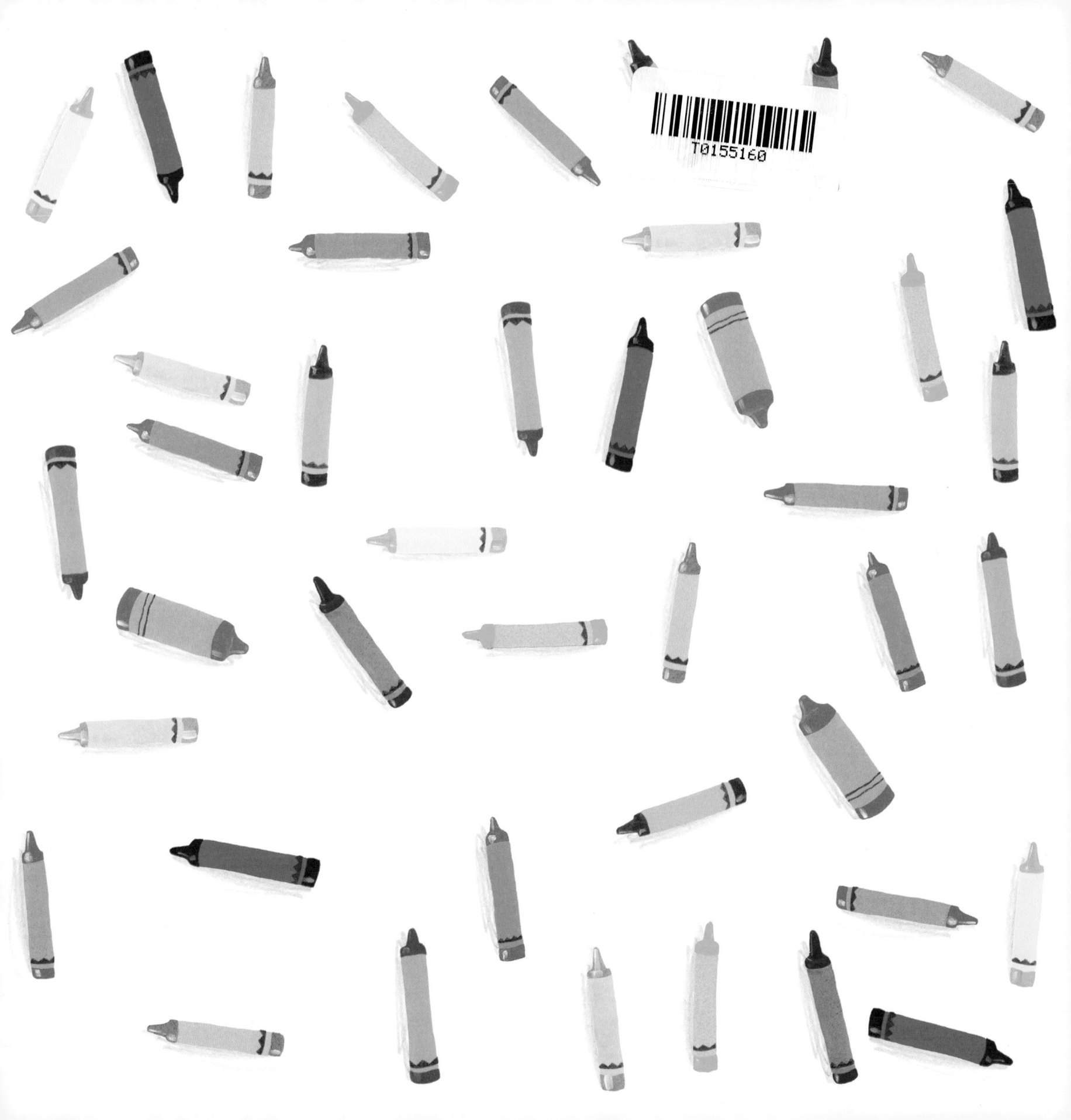

T0155160

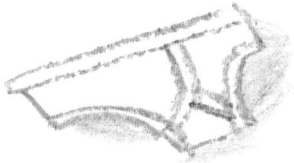

NO. 2

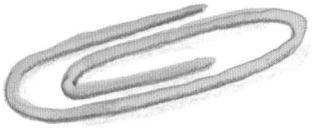

To my parents,
Charles and Charlene Daywalt,
who taught me to always make room for everyone.
—D.D.

For Logan.
—O.J.

The DAY the CRAYONS came HOME

DREW DAYWALT OLIVER JEFFERS

PHILOMEL BOOKS An Imprint of Penguin Group (USA)

One day, Duncan and his crayons were happily coloring together when a strange stack of postcards arrived for him in the mail . . .

Hello from the Rug
484
5
Air Conditioned Suites
The City Hall
2087

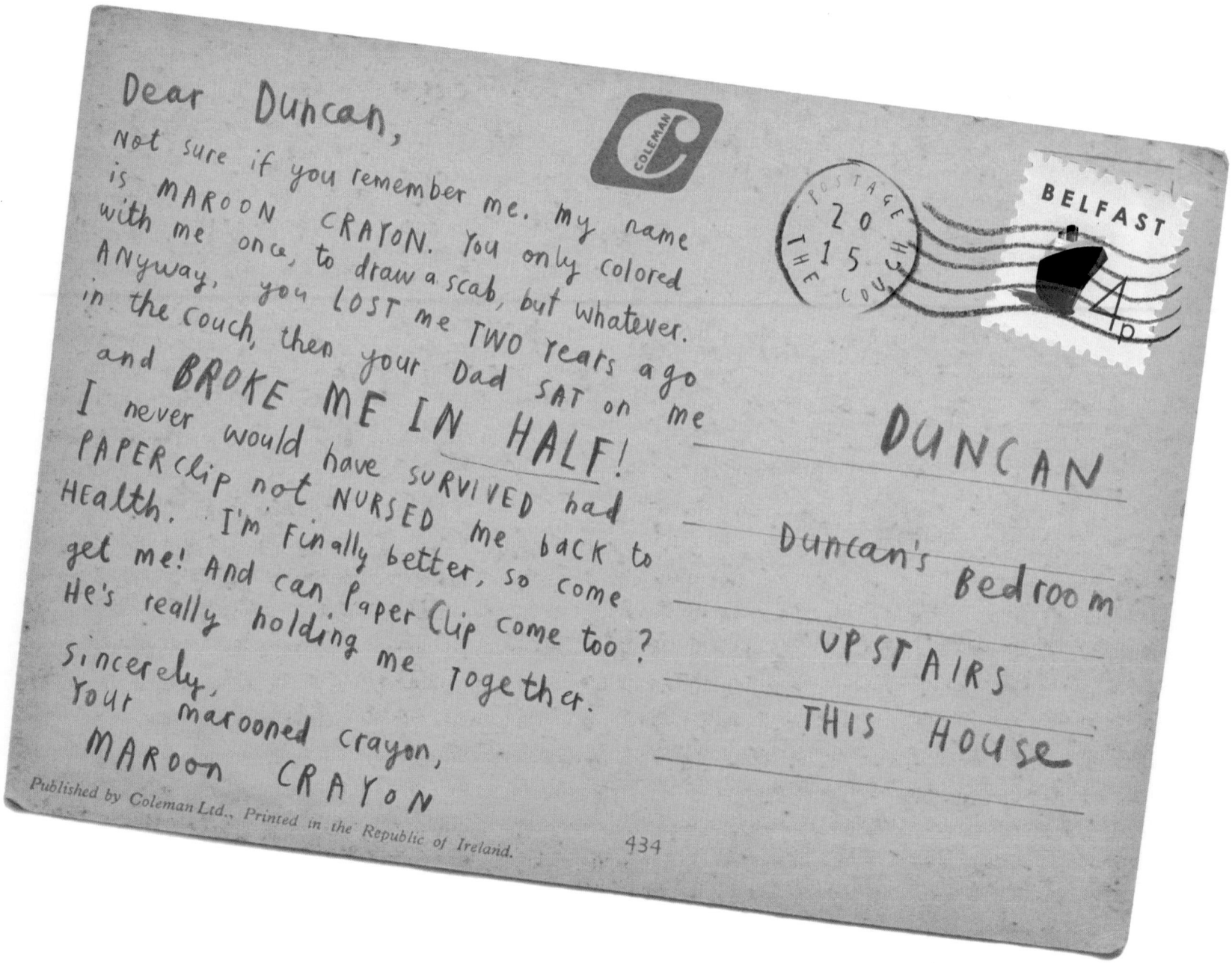

Dear Duncan,

Not sure if you remember me. My name is MAROON CRAYON. You only colored with me once, to draw a scab, but whatever. ANyway, you LOST me TWO years ago in the couch, then your Dad SAT on me and BROKE ME IN HALF! I never would have SURVIVED had PAPERclip not NURSED me back to Health. I'm Finally better, so come get me! And can Paper Clip come too? He's really holding me together.

Sincerely,
Your marooned crayon,
MAROON CRAYON

Published by Coleman Ltd., Printed in the Republic of Ireland.

434

COLEMAN

POSTAGE 20 15 THE COUCH

BELFAST

4p

DUNCAN

Duncan's Bedroom

UPSTAIRS

THIS HOUSE

NOOOOOO...

A MODERN SUPER-HIGHWAY
THRU THE GRANDEUR OF AUTUMN

POSTAGE
IN
SIDE
2015

2¢

DR-29304-B

post card

Dear DUNCAN,
No one likes peas.
No one even likes the color
PEA GREEN. So I'm changing
my name and RUNNING away
to see the WORLD.

Sincerely,
Esteban... the MAGNIFICENT!
(the crayon formerly known as PEA GREEN)

DUNCAN
DUNCAN'S BEDROOM
UPSTAIRS
THIS HOUSE

Sp MADE BY SCAMPI PRESS, INC. NEW YORK

PEA GREEN

Hi, DUNCAN,

RITZ MOTEL

A lovely spot for year 'round recreation

It's me, NEON RED crayon.
REMEMBER that great vacation we had with your Family? Remember how we laughed when we drew a PICTURE of your Dad's SUNBURN? Remember dropping me by the hotel pool when you left? Clearly you do NOT, BECAUSE I'M STILL HERE! How could you miss me? Anyway. After 8 months waiting for you to come get me, I guess I'm walking BACK...

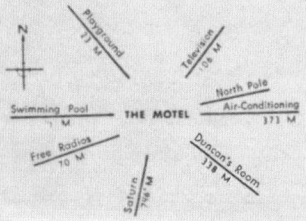

Your left behind Friend,
NEON Red CRAYON

POST CARD

Duncan
Duncan's Room
Duncan's House

NEON RED

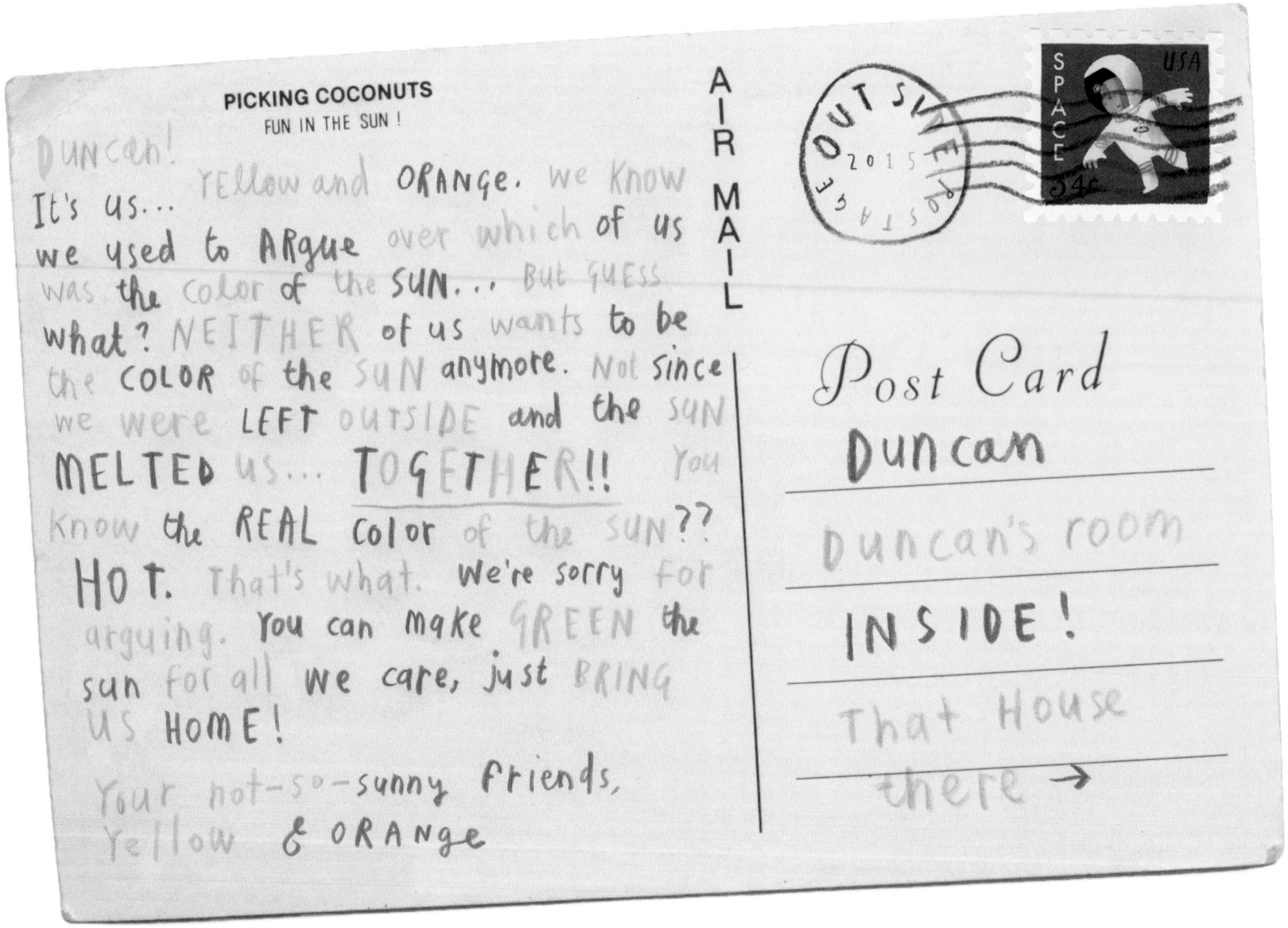

PICKING COCONUTS
FUN IN THE SUN !

AIR MAIL

Duncan!
It's us... Yellow and ORANGE. We know we used to ARgue over which of us was the color of the SUN... BUT GUESS what? NEITHER of us wants to be the COLOR of the SUN anymore. Not since we were LEFT OUTSIDE and the SUN MELTED us... TOGETHER!! You know the REAL color of the SUN?? HOT. That's what. We're sorry for arguing. You can make GREEN the sun for all we care, just BRING US HOME!

Your not-so-sunny friends,
Yellow & ORANGE

OUT SIDE
2015
POSTAGE

USA
SPACE
34¢

Post Card

Duncan

Duncan's room

INSIDE!

That House
there →

Greetings from
NARROWSBURG

Hey Duncan,
I'm sure you don't recognize me... after the horrors I've been through. I think I was... Tan CRAYON? or maybe... Burnt Sienna? I don't know...I can't tell anymore. Have you ever been eaten by a dog and puked up on the living room rug? Because I have... I HAVE BEEN EATEN BY A DOG AND PUKED UP ON THE RUG, Duncan... and it's NOT pretty. Not pretty at all... I'm more carpet fuzz than crayon now. Can you PLEASE bring me back?!

Your UNDIGESTIBLE Friend,
Tan (or possibly Burnt Sienna?) Crayon

P4135

POSTAGE
2015
DOWNSTAIRS

FISH
8¢

Post Card

ADDRESS

Duncan
His Bedroom
UPstairs

NATIONAL MUSEUM OF THE GREAT OUTDOORS
Hall of Fame plaques of natural things.
Attractive exhibits include trees, sand, grass, and bodies of water. Ancient and current history, memorable for adults and children.
POSTAGE
20
15
THE DOOR
6p
BROCCOLI
Post Card
Dearest Duncan,
um... could you please
OPEN the FRONT DOOR?
I still need to see
the world...
sincerely,
Esteban the
magnificent
Duncan
Duncan's Bedroom
UPStairs
This HOUSE
Rev. 1-4

Hey Duncan,
Remember last Halloween we told your little brother there was a GHOST under the BASEMENT stairs? Then we drew that SCARY STUFF on the wall? Sure was funny when he ran SCREAMING, right? But it wasn't so funny when you FORGOT to take me out of the BASEMENT! Please come get me!
I'm kind of... terribly... horrified...

Your scared friend,
GLOW in the DARK crayon

DUNCAN
Duncan's
Bedroom
UPSTAIRS
THIS HOUSE

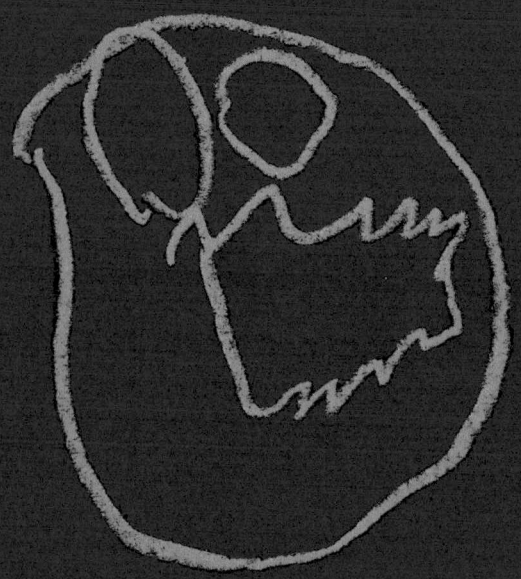

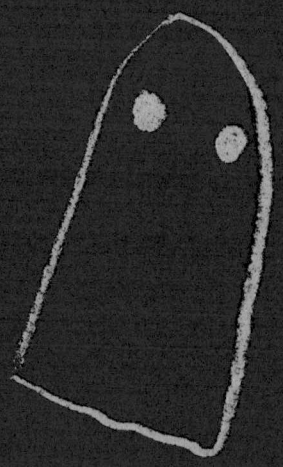

GLOW IN THE DARK

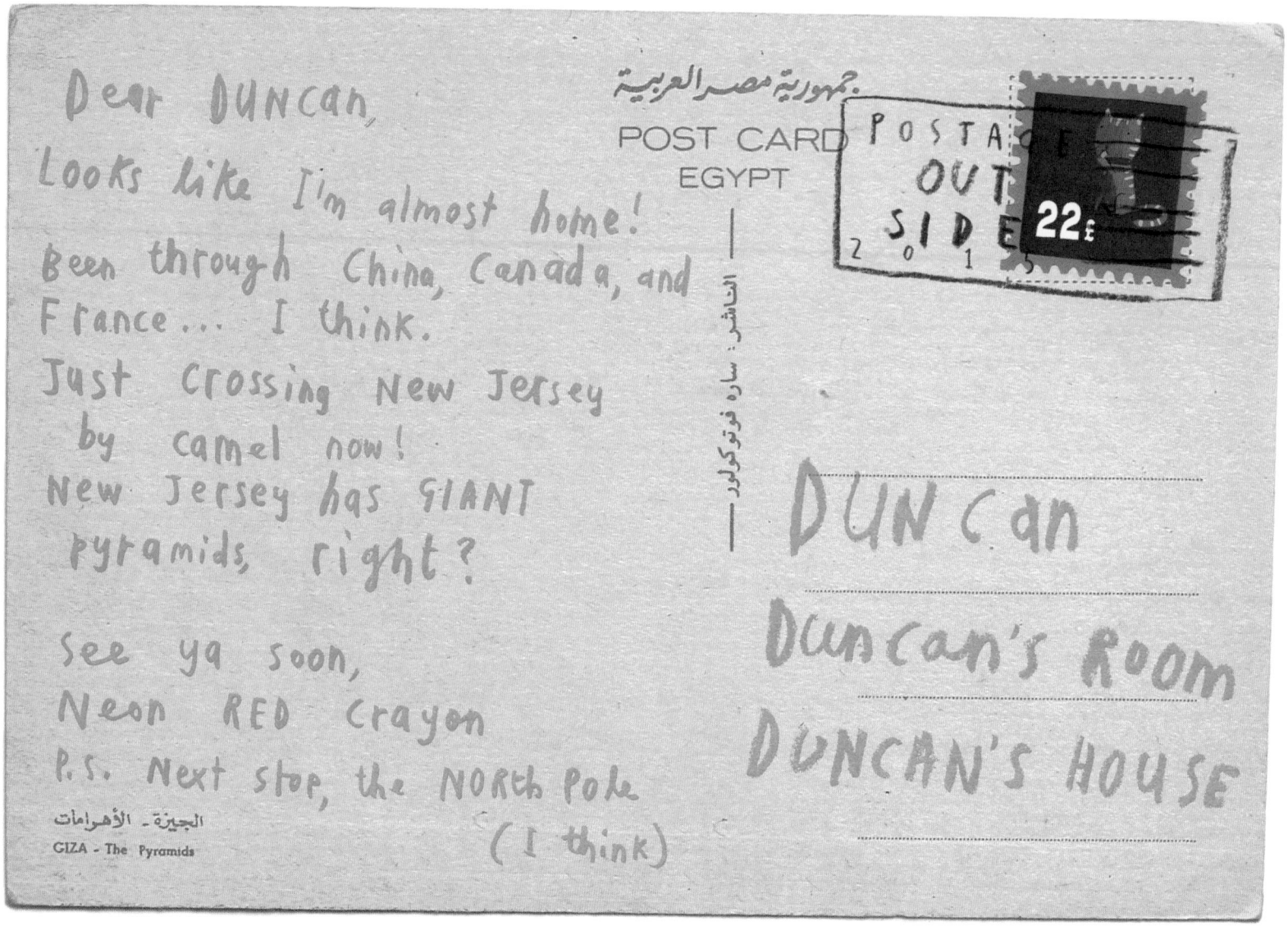

Dear DUNCAN,

Looks like I'm almost home!
Been through China, Canada, and France... I think.
Just crossing New Jersey by camel now!
New Jersey has GIANT pyramids, right?

See ya soon,
Neon RED Crayon
P.S. Next stop, the NORTH Pole (I think)

جمهورية مصر العربية
POST CARD
EGYPT

الناشر: ساره فوتوكولور

الجيزة - الأهرامات
GIZA - The Pyramids

POSTAGE
OUTSIDE
2015
22 £

DUNCAN

Duncan's Room

DUNCAN'S HOUSE

The Land of Gold

Duncan,

Does page 8 of "PIRATE Island" ring a bell? Kind of a big payday for CAPtain GREENBeard there, don't ya think? And NO BRONZE or silver in that pile, huh? I told you it'd make me blunt if you colored each coin INDIVIDUALLY. But would you listen? NOOO. I Also told you those stupid crayon sharpeners NEVER WORK. Did you listen to that? Also NOOOO. NOW I can't color ANYthing at ALL!

Your Pointless FRIend,
GOLD CRAYON

INSIDE POSTAGE 2015

POST CARD

Duncan
DUNCAN'S ROOM
UPstairs

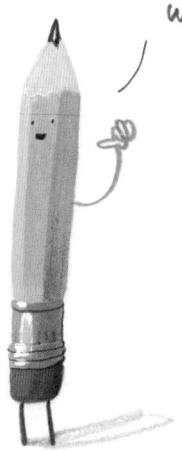

A Haul of Loot

A Bad Day for the Cabin Boy

Dear Duncan,
I've seen the world.
It's rainy.
I'm coming back.
Esteban
the MAGNificent
#72-26 PASSING OF THE STORM...
MULHOLLAND PRESS, INC.
M
P
POSTAGE
2015
THE DOOR
POST CARD
23
EXPLORER
TO Duncan
Duncan's Bedroom
UPStairs
This House

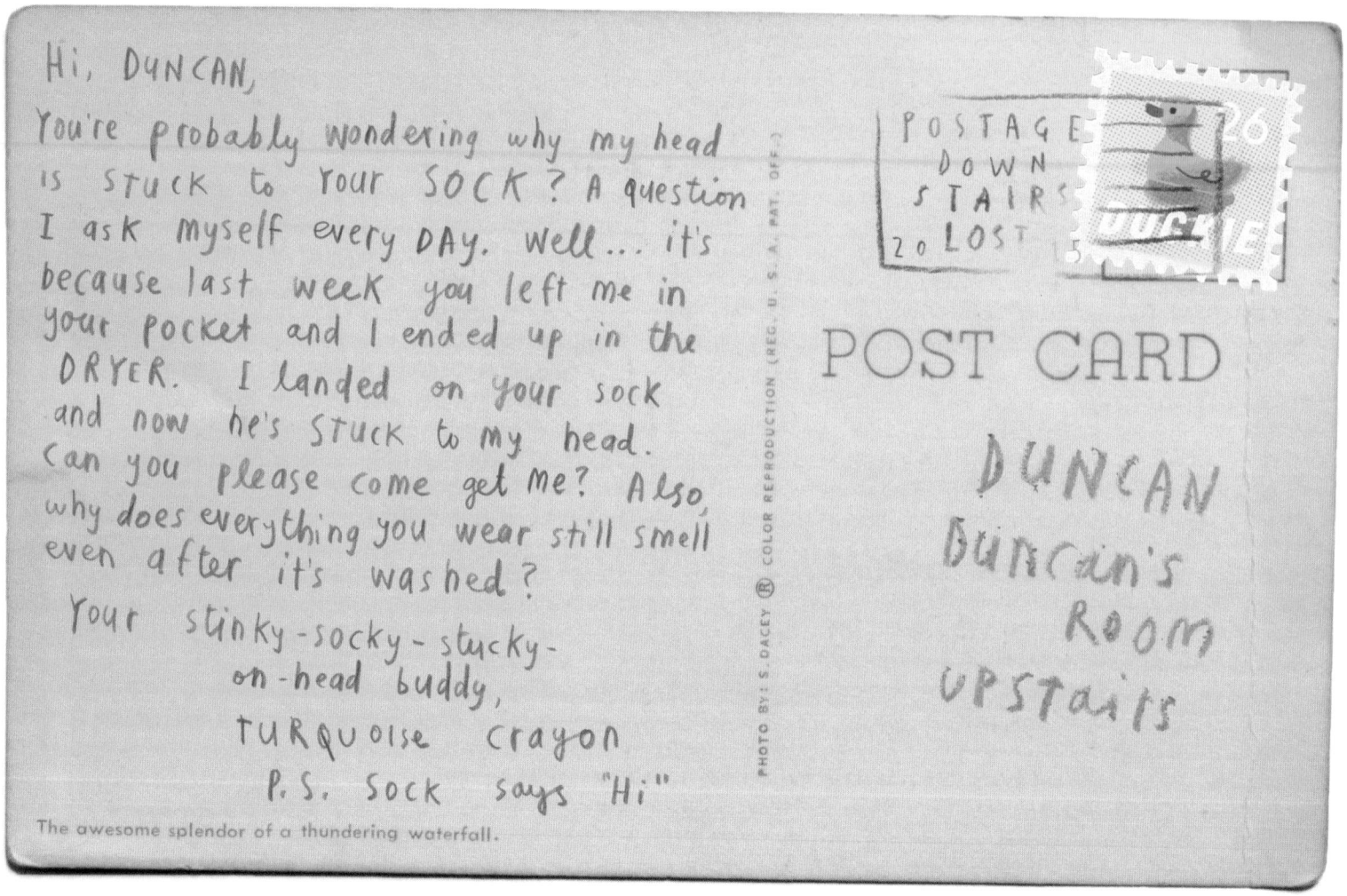
Hi, DUNCAN,
You're probably wondering why my head is STUCK to your SOCK? A question I ask myself every DAY. Well... it's because last week you left me in your pocket and I ended up in the DRYER. I landed on your sock and now he's STUCK to my head. Can you please come get me? Also, why does everything you wear still smell even after it's washed?
Your stinky-socky-stucky-on-head buddy,
TURQUOISE crayon
P.S. Sock says "Hi"
The awesome splendor of a thundering waterfall.
PHOTO BY: S. DACEY ® COLOR REPRODUCTION (REG. U. S. A. PAT. OFF.)
POSTAGE
DOWN
STAIRS
LOST
POST CARD
DUNCAN
Duncan's
Room
UPSTAIRS

TURQUOISE
TELL HIM
I SAID
hi

CARTE POSTALE

Dear Mr. Duncan,

I know I'm not your crayon. I know I belong to your Baby Brother, but I can't TAKE him anymore. In the last WEEK alone he's bitten the Top of my HEAD, put me in the cat's NOSE, drawn on the WALL and tried to color GARBAGE with me! The WORST part is he is a TERRIBLE Artist! I can't tell what his drawings are. Donkeys? Monkeys? DONKEY-MONKEYS? Picasso said every child is an artist, but I dunno. I don't think he met your Brother. Please Rescue me.

Your desperate Friend,

BIG CHUNKY Toddler Crayon

POSTAGE
INSTAGE
2015

l'art orange
97¢

ADRESSE

M. Duncan

Duncan's Room

Upstairs

This House

MY FIRST
CRAYON

SKIING AND A FAST JUMP ALONG THE TRAIL

Duncan,
greetings from the
AMAZON Rain Forest.

making GREat TIME!
I think I'm almost home.

NEON RED crayon

Pub. by Maeve S. White Ridge Enterprise, 04102

Sp MADE BY SCAMPI PRESS

OUTSIDE
2015
04102

4¢
WINTER

DR-28060-B

post card

Duncan
DUNCAN'S Room
DUNCAN'S House

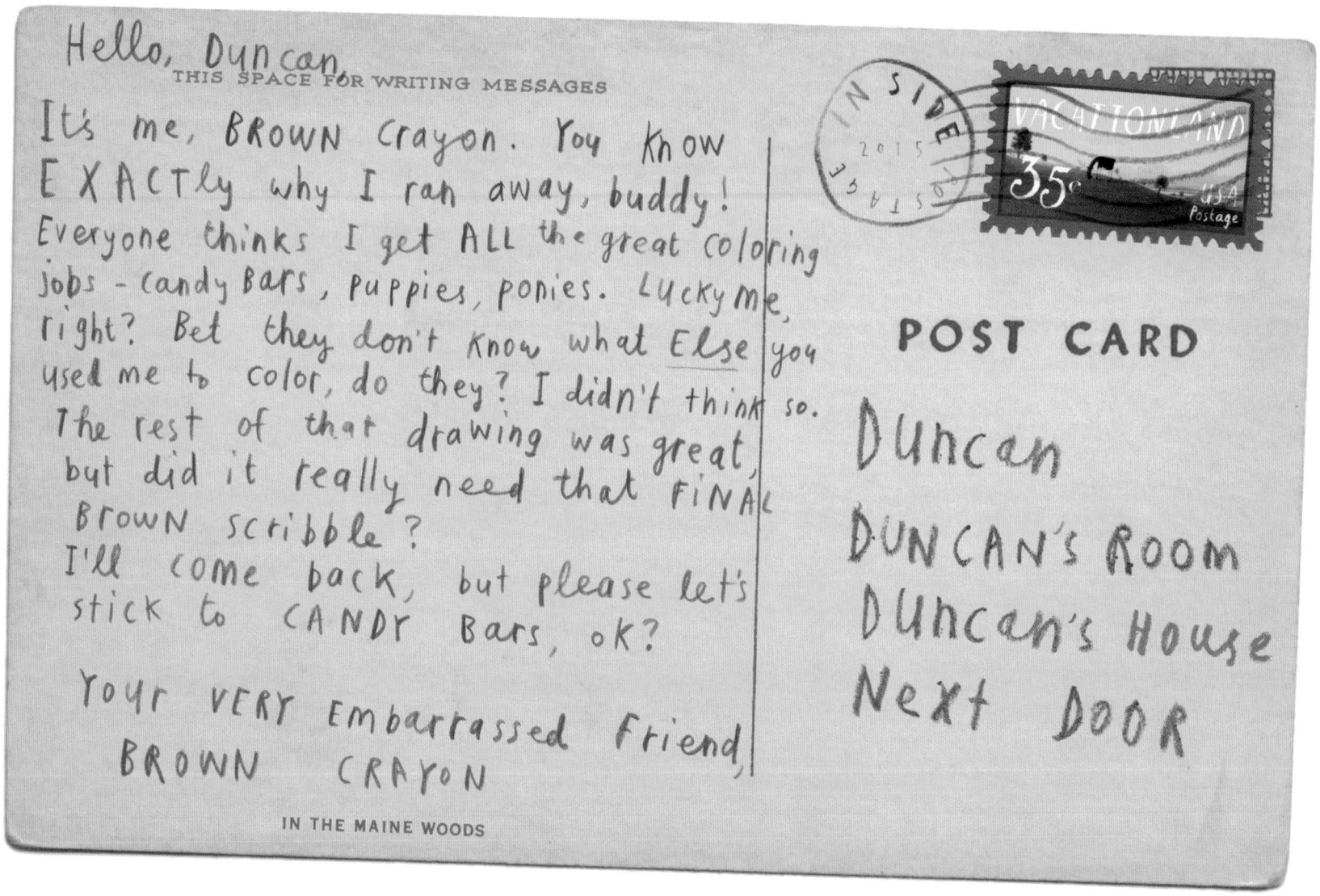
Hello, Duncan,
THIS SPACE FOR WRITING MESSAGES
It's me, BROWN Crayon. You Know EXACTly why I ran away, buddy! Everyone thinks I get ALL the great coloring jobs - candy Bars, puppies, ponies. Lucky me, right? Bet they don't Know what Else you used me to color, do they? I didn't think so. The rest of that drawing was great, but did it really need that FINAL BROWN scribble?
I'll come back, but please let's stick to CANDY Bars, ok?
Your VERY Embarrassed Friend,
BROWN CRAYON
IN THE MAINE WOODS
IN SIDE
POSTAGE
2015
VACATIONLAND
35¢
USA Postage
POST CARD
Duncan
DUNCAN'S ROOM
DUNCAN'S HOUSE
NEXT DOOR

?
BROWN
"BEAR GOES in the WOODS"
by Duncan

Greetings from
NARROWSBURG
Hey Duncan,
I'm sure you don't recognize me...
after the horrors I've been through.
I think I was... Tan CRAYON?
or maybe... Burnt Sienna? I don't
Know... I can't tell anymore. Have
you ever been eaten by a dog and puked
up on the living room rug? Because
I have... I HAVE BEEN EATEN BY A DOG
AND PUKED UP ON THE RUG, Duncan...
and it's NOT pretty. Not pretty at all...
I'm more carpet fuzz than crayon now.
Can you PLEASE bring me back?!
Your UNDIGESTIBLE friend,
Tan (or possibly Burnt Sienna?) Crayon
P4135
POSTAGE
DOWNSTATE
Post Card
ADDRESS
Duncan
His Bed
UPSTA
Dear Duncan,
Not sure if you remember me. My nam
MAROON CRAYON. You only colore
once, to draw a scab, but whatev
you LOST me TWO years a
couch, then your Dad SAT on
BROKE ME IN HALF!
ever would have SURVIVED had
PERclip not NURSED me
alth. I'm Finall
get me
Western
sum
MULHOLLAND PRESS, INC.
POST CAR
TO
Duncan
Duncans Bed
UPSTAIRS
This House
Duncan
Duncans Room
UPSTAIRS
This House
ADRESSE
How
After 8 m
get me, I guess
Your left
NEON Red
CARTE POSTALE
Dear Mr. Duncan,
Next stop the NORTH Pole
(I think)
RED Crayon
GIZA - The Pyramids
DUNCAN'S
Playground
Television
North Pole
Swimming Pool
THE MOTEL
Air-Conditioning
Free Radios
Duncan's Room
Saturn

Duncan was sad to learn of all the crayons he'd lost, forgotten, broken or neglected over the years. So he ran around gathering them up.

But Duncan's crayons were all so damaged and differently shaped than they used to be that they no longer fit in the crayon box.

So Duncan had an idea . . .

He built a place where each crayon would *always* feel at home.

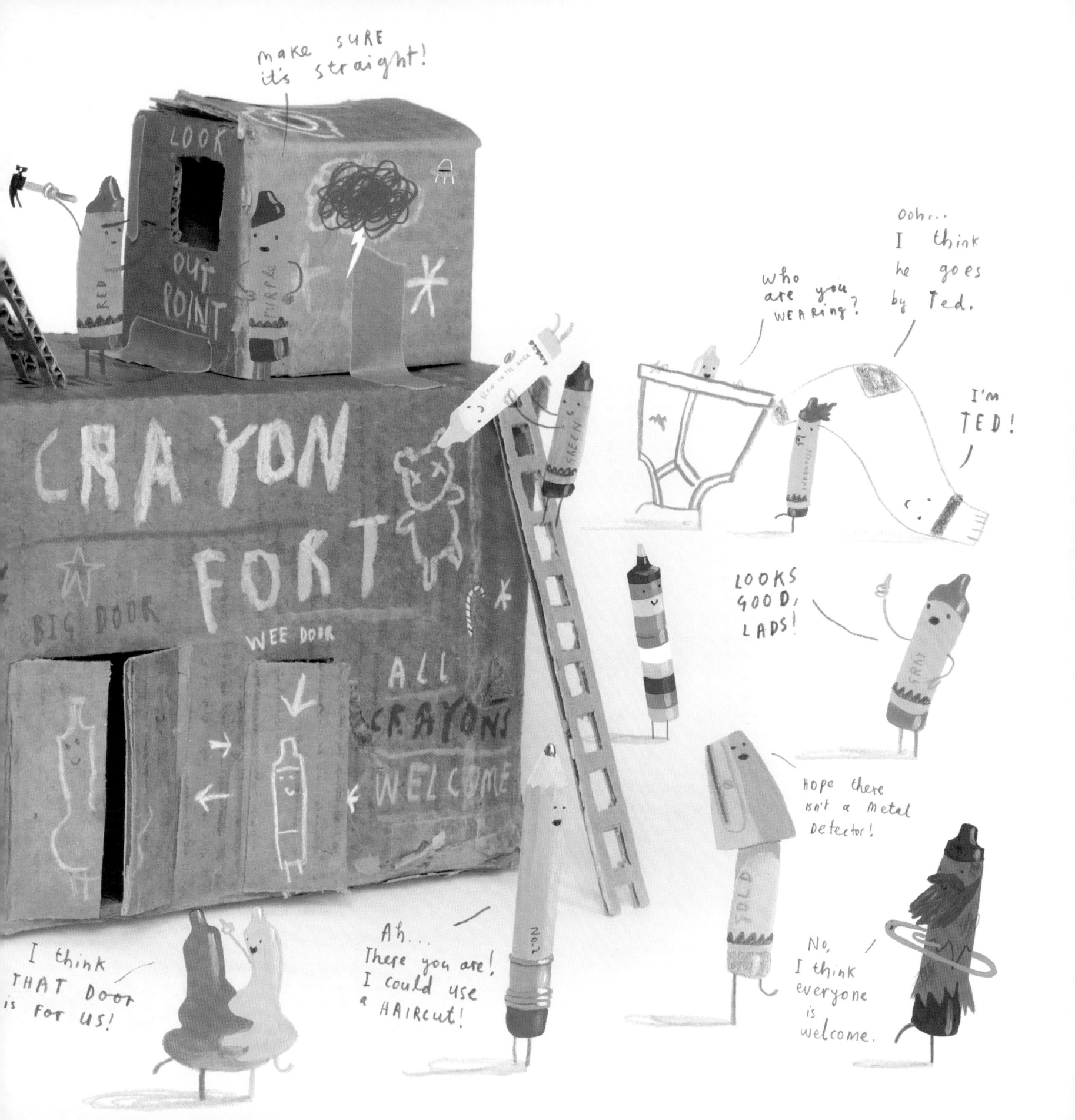
make SURE it's straight!
LOOK OUT POINT
RED
PURPLE
CRAYON FORT
BIG DOOR
WEE DOOR
ALL CRAYONS WELCOME
GLOW IN THE DARK
GREEN
Who are you WEARing?
Ooh... I think he goes by Ted.
I'm TED!
TURQUOISE
LOOKS GOOD, LADS!
GRAY
Hope there isn't a Metal Detector!
GOLD
No, I think everyone is welcome.
No. 2
Ah... There you are! I could use a HAIRcut!
I think THAT Door is FOR US!

ALL
CRAYONS
WELCOME
And then in CLEVELAND...
... I got to hike the
GREAT WALL of CHINA!
ESTEBAN
RED

ALSO BY DREW DAYWALT AND OLIVER JEFFERS:

The Day the Crayons Quit

PHILOMEL BOOKS
Published by the Penguin Group | Penguin Group (USA) LLC
375 Hudson Street, New York, NY 10014

USA | Canada | UK | Ireland | Australia | New Zealand | India | South Africa | China
penguin.com | A Penguin Random House Company

Text copyright © 2015 by Drew Daywalt. Illustrations copyright © 2015 by Oliver Jeffers.
Penguin supports copyright. Copyright fuels creativity, encourages diverse voices, promotes free speech, and creates a vibrant culture. Thank you for buying an authorized edition of this book and for complying with copyright laws by not reproducing, scanning, or distributing any part of it in any form without permission. You are supporting writers and allowing Penguin to continue to publish books for every reader.

Library of Congress Cataloging-in-Publication Data
Daywalt, Drew, author.
The day the crayons came home / by Drew Daywalt ; pictures by Oliver Jeffers.
pages cm Companion book to: The day the crayons quit. Summary: One day, Duncan is happily coloring with his crayons when a stack of postcards arrives in the mail from his former crayons, each of which has run away or been left behind, and all of which want to come home. [1. Crayons—Fiction. 2. Postcards—Fiction. 3. Color—Fiction.] I. Jeffers, Oliver, illustrator. II. Title. PZ7.D3388Dat 2015 [E]—dc23 2015003512

Manufactured in China by RR Donnelley Asia Printing Solutions Ltd.
ISBN 978-0-399-17275-5
10

Edited by Michael Green. Text set in 20-point Mercury Text G1.
The art for this book was made with crayons, the Postal Service, and a cardboard box.

GREETINGS FROM
NEITHER HERE NOR T
PLACE
STAMP
HERE
POST·CARD
AP 10 CRAYON POSTCARD. MADE BY ME
RESTAURANT LOUNGE
THE CRAYON CASTLE
1 Mile west of Duncan's Bedroom. Left out of the Garage.
CRAYON INN MOTEL
Need to Get Out of the Box? Enjoy Our Air Conditioned Suites!
Wish you were here

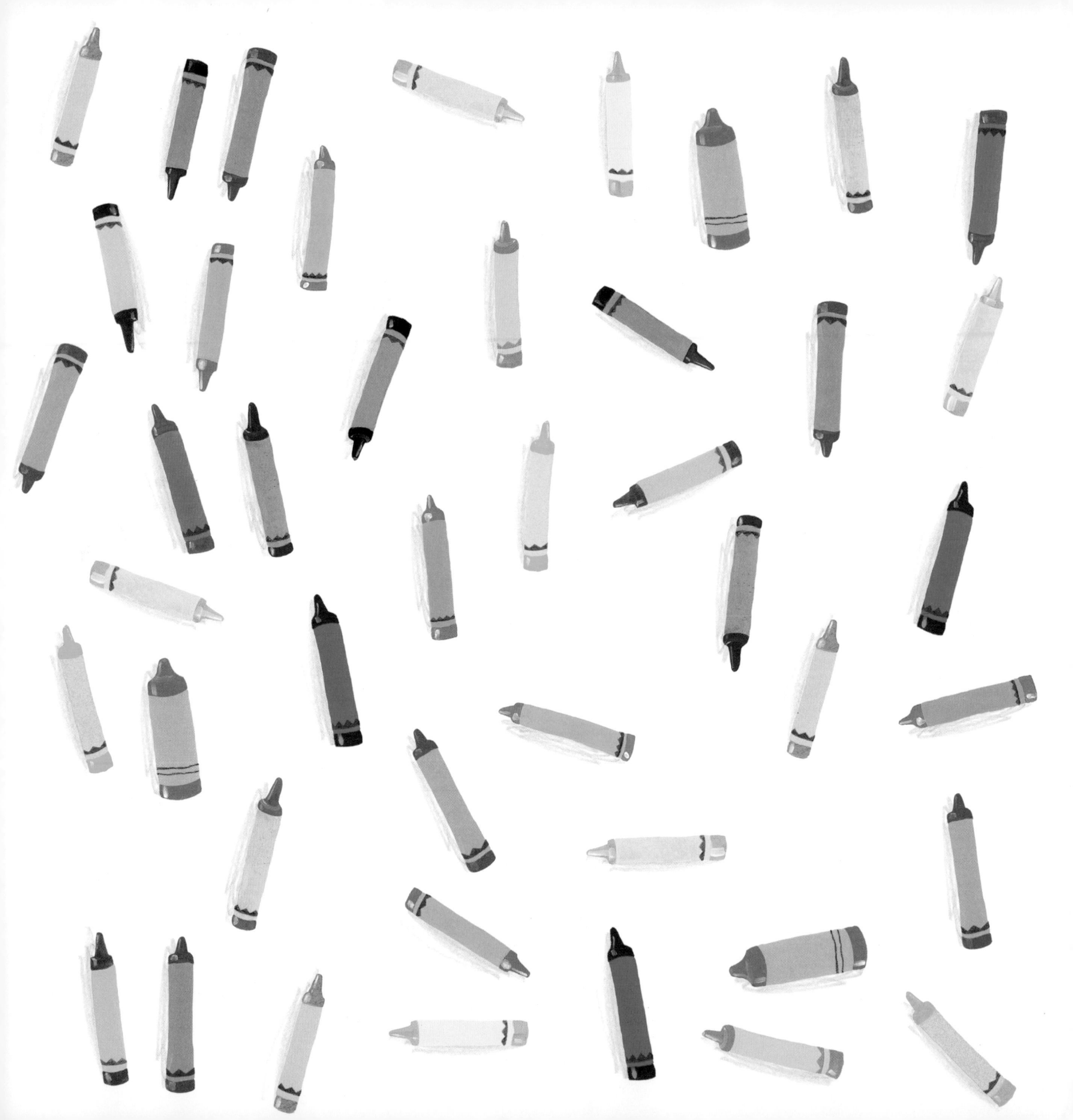